JUDGMENT DAY

JUDGMENT DAY
EVIL INTENTIONS

Chakra, Hiim, Cobra

Judgment Day
Copyright © 2021 by Chakra, Hiim, Cobra. All rights reserved.

No part of this publication may be reproduced, stored in a retrieval system or transmitted in any way by any means, electronic, mechanical, photocopy, recording or otherwise without the prior permission of the author except as provided by USA copyright law.

The opinions expressed by the author are not necessarily those of URLink Print and Media.

1603 Capitol Ave., Suite 310 Cheyenne, Wyoming USA 82001
1-888-980-6523 | admin@urlinkpublishing.com

URLink Print and Media is committed to excellence in the publishing industry.

Book design copyright © 2021 by URLink Print and Media. All rights reserved.

Published in the United States of America

Library of Congress Control Number: 2021901593
ISBN 978-1-64753-651-0 (Paperback)
ISBN 978-1-64753-652-7 (Digital)

15.10.20

Introduction

Some people say there are 10 dimensions what if I told you there are 41?........ The most powerful beings in each universe were sent to the 40th dimension, called judgedom. Judgedom is a universe full of beings that stands for peace. The civilization is ran by eight elite soldiers with powerful weapons symbolizing judgement day. These eight soldiers are ran by the judge, who is the 41st dimension. The other 40 dimensions are inside of the judge, judgedom lies within the heart of the judge. This is the closest dimension to its soul making judgedom very powerful. One day the eight elite soldiers turned on the judge forming a group of eight deadly sins called league of terror causing all types of bad to spread through the body of the judge. Now it's up to the new eight to stop the bad and bring eternal internal peace........This is the messenger I'm radiation

THIS IS JUDGEMENT DAY

Evil intentions

1. **The messenger: (The Temple, Land in Judgedom)** Judgement day I call upon you.

Alexious: (Airbourne, Land in Judgedom)(The waterfall) Aim……little to the left now!! **(Arrow shot)**

Jade: I got it yesss!! did you see that (Looking back)

Alexious: I sure……. (Receives message from messenger) yeah I saw that I saw that meet me here tomorrow same time okay?

Jade: got it **(flies away)**

2. **Elkkan: (The shining Jewels, Land in Judgedom) (The grass fields)**

(Breathing heavily)

The consumer: I can hear you (laughing) cause you're right……here!! Wait **(looking scared)**

Elkkan: don't move **(behind the consumer laughing and hugs him from behind)**

The consumer: (smiling) (both Receives message from messenger)

We have to go we're going to be late

Elkkan: Relax (smiling) you were scared it's okay

The consumer: don't tell spazz

3. **Eca:** (The vibe, Land in Judgedom) (training center) get back!!

(Explosion) are you okay?

Spazz: AAAAHHHHHHH!!!!!! **(Running furiously)**

Perception: I'm good tell me when (behind cover)

Eca: Now!! **(Warps spazz onto silver scope, with staff)**

Monitor: player spazz eliminated

Perception: now take that!!

Silver scope: watch out!! (Shoots through portal) one shot baby

Monitor: player Eca eliminated

Perception: wait….we have to go (Receives message)

Monitor: game over

4. **Footsteps: (Blood moon, Land in Judgedom)(The coffin)** I love you, you do know that?

Ash: of course I know that but your changing (The wife)

Footsteps: I'll make it up to you sweetie I promise will hangout all day and do nothing……we won't even feed the kids tonight.

Ash: (chuckles) now let's not take it that far then I'm really leaving you

Footsteps: (grabs her arm and kisses her) (receives message from messenger)

Ash: so what do you have in mind?

Footsteps: A-Actually (stutters) um…..

Ash: (cuts him off) I already know

Footsteps: love you **(takes off)**

Ash: (sighs)

5. **The messenger: (The temple,Land in judgedom)** judgement day I call upon you welcome judgement day I have a very important message for you Vilekken is trying to take over the 34th to the 39th dimension he must be stopped!

Elkkan: on it! (Messenger shuts down)

The consumer: (Flawless, Land in Judgedom) (The jungle)

Darc: (soldier from army) king can I ask you a question?

The consumer: no (Thinking about mission)

Darc: me and the guys were talking if you consume a girl…… right (Looks back) would you become a girl **(army laughs)**

The consumer: ha ha ha **(Everyone is laughing)**

Darc: (laughing out loud)

The consumer: smack!!!! **(Everyone goes silent)**

Eca: (warps in)

The consumer: now stop!!

Darc: ouchhhhhhh!!! **(Holding head) (runs off, climbs tree)**

Eca: we have to stop Vilekken

The consumer: I'm sorry Darc (walking to Eca) I know I have a plan I think……

Eca: you know what? Meet me at fate and alert the others **(Eca warps) The consumer: (walks to cheer) (Darc and the army talking and laughing) (consumer teleports)**

6. Footsteps: (Blood moon, Land in Judgedom) (The coffin) I don't know guys maybe another time

JUDGMENT DAY

Ash: (screaming out the door) he's not leaving!!

Footsteps: (looks back angrily) she's not letting me leave guys

Spazz: (talks angry) well she's not the judge so…….

Elkkan: (cuts him off) he's always the last one to get ready

The consumer: ironic because he's fast **(chuckles) (Alexious in background talking to ash)**

Alexious: ash I know you understand how this job works. This is our purpose (footsteps arguing with spazz) fate is in our hand Vilekken must be stopped

Perception: I could always just……**(talking to footsteps)**

Footsteps: (looking disappointed)

Silver scope: (smirks)

Alexious: okay I worked my magic footsteps you're allowed to come out to night **(judgement day laughs) (footsteps creates wormhole to (fate)**

7. **Eca: (Fate, Land in Judgedom)(darklands practicing) (in horror form)**

Alexious: (runs up to horror) pop!!! (Blocking scythe with bow arrow) now fight me or return to the underworld (smiling) horror or Eca

Horror: (changes back to Eca)

Eca: (hugs and kisses Alexious) are you cheating on me with horror?

Alexious: maybe or maybe not

Spazz: okay come on let's get this show on the road, how did we make it to judgement day

Eca: Alright here's what we are going to do

8. **Vilekken: (34 Dimension Aquarium, galaxy whirlpool, planet The Reef)** soldiers…enemies up head take cover (explosion underwater) ahhhhhh!! (Armies dying) powww!! **(Vilekken throws whip)**

Aquamarines: retreat!! They have taken the planet **(Aquamarines vanishes)**

Vilekken: victory is ours!! (Army celebrates) yeahhhh!!

Vilekken soldier: my lord we have detected the water gem, on a planet called waterfall **(looking at a screen)**

Vilekken: good we shall move tomorrow **(army celebrating in background)**

Aquamarine soldier: (In a galaxy called whirlpool, planet waterfall)(The sand castle) I need to speak to the king!! **(thousands of soldiers appearing)**

King Aquarius: (The sand castle) (holding daughter)

Queen flow: what are you and Heidi up to my king? (happy) give me her **(both laughing)**

Aquamarines: (bursts through the door ruffly) King were under attack

!!

King Aquarius: they're here gear up and prepare for battle (walks to room and holds water gem) Judgement day I call upon you welcome judgement day I have a very important message for you. Vilekken is trying to take over the 34th to the 39th dimension he must be stopped!

King Aquarius: (puts water gem back)(using telekinesis to call LT.

Gills)

LT.Gills: Sir what is going on the reef has been conquered. Is this who I think it is?

King Aquarius: yes, it's them…The time has come! The plan B is in affect.

LT. Gills: affirmative

King Aquarius: (kisses family and suits up)

9. Eca: (Fate,land in Judgedom)(underworld) okay the dimension we are going to is all water

Perception: this should be fun

Elkkan: so do you think we should

Spazz: (cuts her off) I say we go and fight

Footsteps: okay we warp there

Alexious: Exactly, and Elkkan makes suits for us allowing us to breathe underwater

Eca: and stop vilekken

Spazz: I'm down

The consumer: lets get ready we're running out of time**(judgement day prepares)**

Eca: (walks from team and pulls out platinum ball whispers under breath)

Sunlight: (walks up) I'll pray for your return **(disappears)**

Elkkan: everyone do not take off suits when we enter the Aquarium they say waters are forbidden from outsiders

Spazz: I'm pumped ahhhhhhh!!!

Eca: here we go **(judgement day warps)**

10.vilekken: set up base! Any survivors are prisoners **(smacks aquamarine survivor with whip and kills him)**

SGT. Smoke vilekken army soldier: yes sir!

Judgement day: (warps outside the planet Reef)

The consumer: woah….(Looking around curiously)

Perception: (swims over to dead Aquamarine) can you hear me?

Soldier, I am perception of judgement day can you hear me?!

(Grabbing soldier)

Silver scope: he must be dead we have to move!!

Perception: no! Something is wrong….**(thinking deeply)**

Spazz: (turning orange) he's obviously dead!

Perception: no we need intel…

Eca: perception don't!

Perception: (lifts helmet up) can you hear me now?

Aquamarine: (opens eyes wide in shock)(whispering) perception?......

Perception: how do you know my name?

Aquamarine: you are…..**(dies)**

Perception: (cries) what? I'm what? **(Tears turning into a bubble leading the way to vilekken)**

Perception: follow the bubble

The consumer: are you okay? **(Elkkan looks back at the two)**

Perception: yes thank you

The consumer: don't worry it's going to be okay be strong **(perception smiles looking at the consumer)**

Elkkan: guys come on we need to move

Perception: (gets flashes of her past as she swims to vilekken) my head I feel funny

Elkkan: come on I gotcha (the others swim ahead) take your time, it's beautiful here

Perception: yeah, hey I think….

Eca: look!! up head you guys **(planet Reef)**

Spazz: ha ha ha ha!! Let the party began

11. **Vilekken: (planet Reef)** I want it taller!!

SGT. Smoke: yes my lord, everyone together push ahhhhhh!!!

Vilekken: one day you will have a throne like mines….

Spazz: (Eca warps him to reef) ahhhhhhhhh!!!!!! Boommmm!!! **(Destroying enemies with his brass knuckles)(giving him unlimited powers of rage)**

Vilekken: attack!! **(Army dying)**

Silver scope: Vilekken is trying to escape

Spazz: not on my watch Ahhhhhh!!! Boommmm!!! **(Vilekken and spazz fight)**

Elkkan: (fighting army) slip slip! (Controlling the elements in their body) above!! **(Throws enemies up)** (her diamond heart enhances her ability)

Alexious: I got them!! **(flies up and hits enemies with exploding arrows) (the ability of magic bow arrow)**

Perception: scope there coming to you **(controls enemies mind with her necklace)**

Silver scope: one shot baby **(gets a collateral with his dual pistols)(giving him the ability to have everyone's weakness)**

Elkkan: (creates explosion) (horror jumps out of it)

Horror: (horror scream killing his enemies around him) (rips enemies apart) (staff/scythe giving him the ability to control life and death)

The consumer: not today (laughing) (throws spear letting it fight for him) (giving him the ability to give) I am the greatest judgement you'll ever fine

Elkkan: oh please **(drowns her enemies)**

Consumer: what? I'm untouchable (wraps tail around enemies throat) smack!!!

Silver scope: I saw that, footsteps now!**(shoots bullet that stops enemies from moving)**

Footsteps: (runs threw army) (runs so fast past the enemies there souls come out their bodies) (his shoes gives him infinite speed) (Sucking the blood out of enemies)

Spazz: take this (throws Vilekken) boom!!, you will bow to me **(throws Vilekken again)**

Vilekken: (laughs) you bow to me **(uppercuts spazz into the air)(whip floats to his hand and puts whip around his neck, slamming spazz back and forth)**

Vilekken: soldiers we must get water gem!! Smoke stay!, the rest come with me.**(he leaves planet)(heading to planet waterfall)**

Horror: he's getting away!! **(Jumps up with scythe spinning it causing a force shield around the planet)**

The consumer: watch me work ladies (consumes all the water off the planet allowing them to walk) he got away all because of Spazz!!

Spazz: what!! No no we can go right now pretty boy **(turning red)**

Eca: relax guys

Elkkan: I dare you to touch him **(stands in spazz face)**

Alexious: focus he's going after the gem

Silver scope: you guys go head I'll watch here (millions of soldiers running up to them)

Eca: okay, you heard the man

The consumer: this isn't over **(talking to spazz)**

Spazz: play with your life ha ha ha ha **(judgement day walks threw portal) (heading to planet waterfall to stop Vilekken)**

Silver scope: here we go **(runs to the millions of soldiers) (shoots a 1,000 soldiers, then falls to ground and shoots a random shot in the air)**

King Aquarius: (suiting up, heads to balcony looking at civilians board submarine) (planet waterfall) (the sand castle)

Aquamarine soldier: your highness Vilekken army has been attacked by some type angels of some sort

King Aquarius: they are good allies of mine, they are here to help

Queen Flow: (Heidi crying) sh…..it's going to be ok baby **(cradles her)(LT. Gills gesturing civilians to line up and board submarine)**

Aquamarine soldier: your highness come aboard

Flow: (hands soldier the baby)

Aquamarine soldier: enemies approaching from the sky! Come on Queen

Aquarius: (yelling from balcony) flow get on the fucking submarine!

Queen flow: go without me!

LT.Gills: grab her!

Aquamarine soldiers: we have to go gills it's her choice!

Queen flow: that's an order!

Vilekken soldier: (appears goes for the submarine that Heidi is aboard but is randomly assassinated)

Queen flow: what the? Aquarius help me?

King Aquarius: I'm coming sweetie, run!

Vilekken: (warps out the sky throwing whip around Queen flow neck instantly killing her)

Vilekken: charge!!! **(Army charges to the aquamarine soldiers and to the sand castle)**

Aquamarines: Ahhh!!! **(Charging Vilekken army)**

Aquarius: (jumping down steps breaks out the door and sees his wife dead) no!!!!!!!!! Flow please…. No **(cries silently)**

Vilekken: there's the king! Soldiers let's finish this!

Aquarius: (looking up furiously) aquamarines!! I want his head

Aquamarine soldier: we need reinforcements King **(gets grabbed and killed)**

Aquarius: (screams and sends shockwave killing dozens of Vilekken soldiers) ahhhh!!

Judgement day: (warps into waterfall)(the sand castle)

JUDGMENT DAY

The consumer: I think we made a wrong turn

Spazz: or a right turn

Elkkan: let's do this!

Footsteps: enemies ahead!(scene flips to Aquarius)

King Aquarius: ahhhhh!!! **(Stabs 10 soldiers to death and charges at Vilekken)**

Vilekken: (whips king Aquarius face and knocks him out)

Aquamarine soldier: (goes for a strike but Vilekken teleports inside the castle)

Vilekken: at last the first peace to my puzzle! (Laughs deviously…)

Ha ha ha ha! **(Disappears)(scene switches to Aquarius)**

Vilekken army: (chains Aquarius to death) the king is dead! Yeah!!

(Disappears)

Aquamarine soldiers : no!!!

Aquamarine soldier: where did they go? (Scene switch to judgement day)(somewhere farther away from the sandcastle)

Horror: (sends out black knight army out his scythe) attack!!

Footsteps: (runs through vilekken army)

Elkkan: (causes meteor shower) take that!

Spazz: ahhhh!!! **(Pounds ground causing a earthquake)**

The consumer: the waters falling!! I think it's raining or something

Alexious: the Vilekken army is disappearing

The consumer: what in the name of the heart is going on

Horror: they killed Aquarius

Wounded Aquarius: they are on their way to the 35th dimension (coughs) they have the water gem, get off the planet this is the end…**(dies next to wife)**

Perception: (sheds a glowing teardrop bubble)(Sky cracks open)

Spazz: the sky is falling!!

Horror: (warps everyone out of the planet) (planet caves in and floods into the universe vanishing)

The consumer: that was a close one..(Judgement day floating in aquarium)

Footsteps: tell me about it

The messenger: judgement day I call upon you.

Eca: Let's see what radiation has to say

Elkkan: hurry let's move….Eca

12. **Vilekken:** (35th **melody universe, octave Galaxy planet of poets**) **Vilekken:** (**appears in pitch black**) soldiers I have a song to sing (**trumpet is passed to him**) (**plays the notes**) (**a tree like universe appears**)

Vilekken army: victory will soon be ours!!!

Vilekken: we must get the dying seed

Vilekken army soldier: yes my lord

Vilekken: soldiers we move!! (**Moves towards the planet of poets**)

13. **The messenger:** (**The temple, land in Judgedom**) judgement day you must go to the 39th dimension Vilekken must be stopped or the balance of life will be thrown off (**messenger leaves**)

The consumer: anybody wanna party at my house?

Footsteps: really, wow

Alcxious: I don't know how you deal with him

The consumer: what?

Perception: (chuckles)

Elkkan: what's so funny?

Spazz: all it takes is one punch **(talking about consumer)**

The consumer: I will kick your

Alexious: (cuts him off) I need a drink

Silver scope: I'm going to the vibe

Eca: to the vibe everyone **(The vibe is a land in Judgedom full of entertainment)**

14. **Vilekken: (planet of poets, octave galaxy) (35th dimension)** today your King will be defeated **(standing in a arena)**

King harpton: I wish not to fight you, but I will do whatever to protect my universe (talking from balcony)

Kings son: dad let me take him

Vilekken: ha ha ha ha this will be fun

Queen banshee: (the wife) I want his head, I love you **(nervous energy)**

King harpton: I love you more, no problem **(walks in arena) (the whole universe is watching this battle)**

Vilekken: (holding arms out looking at the sky) (his army praises him)

King harpton: fight well

Vilekken: save the formality **(crowd goes quiet as they stand face to face)**

Queen banshee: (screams to the top of her lungs) I want his head!!

(Eyes filled with emotions)

Vilekken: (runs up jump swing his whip) ahhhhh!!! **(Crowd goes wild)**

(Scene changes to judgement day at the vibe)

Alexious: round them up (drinking) I feel great

Spazz: where has this side been? (Laughs) round them up

Alexious: (laughing) keep them coming I wouldn't want any to go to waste

Spazz: I like her yeahhhhhh!!!!

(Scene flips to vilekken vs King harpton)

Vilekken: your weak **(fighting)**

King harpton: (blocks whip with a sword of energy) I will never give up

(crowd cheering)

(Scene changes to judgement day at the vibe)

Elkkan: (sitting at a table alone)(watching perception inner act)

The consumer: **(walks up from behind) (talks in her ear)** hey! what are you doing? **(Hugging her as he's sitting down)**

Elkkan: nothing (smiling) promise me you won't do anything wreck less

The consumer: (smiling) I'm the best (she hits him in the arm) ouchhhh!!!

Elkkan: I'm serious **(looking into his eyes)**

The consumer: I promise

Elkkan: love you

The consumer: love you too, know give me some monkey love **(kisses her all over her face playing, both laughing)**

(Scene flips to vilekken vs King harpton)

Vilekken: (kicks King harpton right in the stomach) this is to easy

(laughing)

King harpton: (drops sword and tackle vilekken to the ground) ahhhh!! **(Over top of him punching him to death)**

(Scene changes to judgement day at the vibe)

Footsteps: my wife always yelling at me, can you do this for me can you get the kids clothes **(talking to a random civilian at the vibe)**

Civilian: is she black?

(Scene flips to vilekken vs King harpton)

King harpton: (stands up over vilekken) you die (picks up sword) ahhhhhhhhh!!!! **(Crackkkkk!!)**

(Scene changes to judgement day at the vibe)

Silver scope: even though I always seem serious, it's because I have faith in us we can do this

Eca: you think so? **(looking at Alexious drink)**

Alexious: (walks over to Eca) excuse me boys, may I have this dance my love

Eca: (dancing with Alexious) what are you doing?

Alexious: celebrating

Eca: (chuckles) celebrating? What we did terrible today you and I both know

Alexious: I'm pregnant **(smiling looking into his eyes)**

Eca: say what now?

(Scene flips to vilekken vs King harpton)

Vilekken: (crowd goes quiet) crack!!!! (King harpton arms falls off) (whip floating behind harpton) (Vilekken stands up whip floats to his hand) this is the end for you(King harpton drop to his knees) watch your King as he dies!!! **(Vilekken army cheers)**

King harpton: (looks to his family) I love you **(crack!!!)** **(King harpton head falls off)**

Vilekken: (smiles) (and takes the dying seed out of King harpton weapon and flees)

(Scene changes to judgement day at the vibe)

Eca: (dancing with soon to be wife)

(Scene flips to King harpton death)

Queen banshee: (drops to floor eyes filled with water) (gets up runs to King harpton body) nooooo!!!!**(screams and destroys the whole universe killing everyone who exist in it)**

(Scene changes to judgement day at the vibe)

Eca: (Alexious and Eca kiss)

The messenger: judgement day I call upon you…

Spazz: let's move out…..

15. Vilekken: (39th dimension paradise)(gates of absolute) (sun shinning) let's hurry soldiers I can taste victory!

Vilekken army soldier: my lord, the gates of absolute is up ahead!

Vilekken: ah…..at last paradise! Soldiers! We are after one thing and that is the key of existence, we take the key we control the judge!

Vilekken army: yes, lord Vilekken!

Vilekken: (walks up to the two guards standing at the gates of absolute

Guard 1: identification please.

Vilekken: my name is lord vilekken I am here to see an old friend of mine

Guard 2: lord vilekken we can not let you in! Alert the creator!

Guard 1: (flies over gate)

Guard2: (follows)

Vilekken: (grabs guard 2 by neck with whip) (killing him) get ready soldiers! **(Cracks lock open with whip)**

Guard 1: creator, they are here!

Liberator: father I shall end this

Creator: no my son, we work as a team, angels assemble **(Angels rising)**

(Scene flips to judgement day)

The messenger: **(The temple, land in Judgedom)** judgement day vilekken is in the 39th dimension he is after the key of existence stop him and this will be over. This will be our last chance judgement day.

Perception: we won't let you down I assure you **(judgement day warps to terror, land in Judgedom) (the Black Sea)**

(Scene flips to creator vs vilekken)

Creator: Angels we fight till we conquer! You will be ran by prince liberator! **(Vilekken army appears)**

Liberator: Vilekken… You have a corrupted soul… One that could be fixed… You are originally benevolent you….

Vilekken: shhhh,(cuts him off) benevolent… Describes you…. I am flat out opposite of such a word, ha ha ha ha!!!

Creator: vilekken! This ends now!

Liberator: father, this doesn't have to end in blood, for I shall follow a peaceful path.

Vilekken: your son is weak, just like you!

Liberator: what did you call me?

Vilekken: (raises whip) you're a pathetic weakling!

Liberator: (turns into the dilator and grows humongous)

Vilekken: (looks surprised) attack!!!

Vilekken army: ahhhhh!!!!

Creator: Angels, release arrows!

Vilekken army soldier: watch out arrows in coming **(wis, wis, wis,wis)(sound effects of arrows flying past)**

Vilekken army soldier: man down! **(Gets hit through neck with arrow)**

Creator: ground soldiers attack vilekken army, Angels lay covering fire

Liberator: (still in dilator form) I'll take vilekken **(runs through vilekken army to vilekken)**

Vilekken: (wraps liberators legs with whip) ha ha ha ha!

Liberator: (falling) whoa!!! Boom!! **(Crushing a lot of soldiers from each side) (liberator shrinks back to normal size) (Scene flips to judgement day at terror)(the Black Sea)**

Perception: team we got this!

Eca: (in horror form) this is it guys

The consumer: and girls

Spazz: save his heart I'm a little hungry **(talking about vilekken)**

Eca: let's go! **(Warps judgement day to paradise) (Scene switch to liberator)**

Liberator: (trying to heal soldiers) ugh... I'm... Weak....

Vilekken: your finished **(swings whip at liberator)**

Creator: **(slices whip in half)** sling!!! **(With a flying sword) (armies fighting in the background)**

Vilekken: (whip grows back) prepare for beating!

Creator: bring it.....

Vilekken: (strikes)

Creator: (turns sword into shield blocking whip) (trips over dead body)

Vilekken: Neal before me peasant fore I am lord vilekken! **(Strikes)**

Creator: (flips out of the way) (shoots energy drain Ray out sword at vilekken)

Vilekken: (dodges Ray) miss!! Now take this **(whip turns into a huge cobra)**

Creator: (fighting snake)

Liberator: (running up to touch snake which would turn it good instead of evil)

Vilekken: no!!! **(Tackles liberator just before he touches snake)(they fist fight it out)**

(Snake whip choking creator out)

(Portal opens)

Spazz: ahhhhh!!!(comes crashing down) boom! (Lands on snake picks it up swings it around and throws it) judgement day has arrived!!!

(Punches 10 enemies heads off)

Vilekken: (whip flies to vilekken in regular form) (judgement day comes through portal) judgement day we meet again!

Eca: vilekken, this is your final warning drop the whip.

Spazz: prince, King, get up, we have a war to finish

Liberator: father, he's not moving**! (trying to heal creator)**

Spazz: the snake must of killed him kid…. I'm sorry kid….

Creator: cough! Cough!

Spazz: creator, I am spazz of judgement day. I need the key.

Creator: (gives up key) stop him….,

Spazz: don't worry we will, kid you got a name?

Liberator: I am Liberator, the prince of paradise

Spazz: okay, lib keep your father alive stay with him

Liberator: affirmative

Creator: hey…. Good luck!

Spazz: (cracks a smile then runs into battle explosively)

Horror: footsteps now!

Footsteps: (runs towards vilekken)

Vilekken: (trips footsteps with his whip!!)

Footsteps: (flips out of control hits his head knocking him self out)

The consumer: how did he move that fast?

Elkkan: he didn't his whip did

Silver scope: watch out (shoots whip as it attempted to hit elkkan) (Whip smacks bullet and hits silver scope in the stomach) boom!!

Horror: (staff turns into scythe) (creates a dark tornado)

Vilekken: (splits tornado in half with whip)

The consumer: (consumes tornado) you can't hurt me! Vilekken your done

Vilekken: (whips a black hole under consumer)(consumer falls threw it and ends up unconscious falling from the sky)** ha!

Spazz: (runs up!) I have the key! (**Pulls out the key**)

Horror: good job spazz! Put it away!

Elkkan: monkey no! (**Flies to his falling body and catches him**)(**eyes filled with anger and sadness**)

Vilekken: (grabs key with whip)

Horror: spazz! What part of put key away….

Spazz: I'm sorry guys! (**Turns purple**)

(**Charges with horror at vilekken**)

Horror: (strikes blade at vilekken, misses)

Spazz: (swings at vilekken, misses)

Alexious: silver scope, stay with me, hang in there

Silver scope: where is perception?

Vilekken: (wraps horror and spazz with whip)

Alexious: horror! (**Shoots arrow at vilekken**)

Vilekken: (catches arrow)

Alexious: what the? (**Then she gets struck by vilekken soldier**)

Horror: (tied down) Alexious!!!

Spazz: (turning a neon red)(tied down slightly breaking out)

Vilekken: victory is ours!

Vilekken army: yeah!!!

Vilekken: tonight I hold three precious items! The water gem! The dying seed and the key of existence!

Vilekken army: yeah!!!!

Vilekken army soldier: my lord here is the creator and his son They are prisoners now!

Spazz: you'll never win….. **(turning white)**

Horror: the judge will over rule you…..

Vilekken: accept defeat **(laughs deviously)**

(Puts items together)

Creator: no! **(explosion Shockwave after vilekken puts items together)**

Vilekken: **(items disappear from his hands after putting them together)** what is happening? **(Looking confused)**

(Screen backs out)

(The black sea, a land in Judgedom)

Judgement day: **(laughing)** **(looking into a glowing teardrop bubble)**

Perception: that's the best part I swear it is!!

Spazz: ha ha ha!!! Wait rewind the part to consumers death. It was Hilarious!

Perception: you like that don't you **(laughing)**

The consumer: first of all that's impossible I'm the greatest, second of all spazz live longer than me....nah....

Perception: I got him good! (Talking about vilekken)

(Screen moves around the room of teardrops) (goes back into vilekken bubble)

Vilekken: (surrounding goes black) (vilekken open his eyes) where the hell am I ?

The reaper: (paranormal voice) Vilekken… **(whispering)**

Vilekken: I can't move, wait, no let's talk about this

The reaper: judgement day has come!

Vilekken : ahhhhhhhhhhh!!!!!!!!!!!

www.ingramcontent.com/pod-product-compliance
Lightning Source LLC
LaVergne TN
LVHW021744060526
838200LV00052B/3453